Dear Readers:

Real adventure is many things—it's danger and daring and sometimes even a struggle for life or death. From competing in the Iditarod dogsled race across Alaska to sailing the Pacific Ocean, I've experienced some of this adventure myself. I try to capture this spirit in my stories, and each time I sit down to write, that challenge is a bit of an adventure in itself.

You're all a part of this adventure as well. Over the years I've had the privilege of talking with many of you in schools, and this book is the result of hearing firsthand what you want to read about most—power-packed adventure and excitement.

You asked for it—so hang on tight while we jump into another thrilling story in my World of Adventure.

Gary Paulsen's
World of Adventure

Time Benders

MACMILLAN CHILDREN'S BOOKS

First published 1997 by Bantam Doubleday Dell, USA

First published in the UK 1999 by Macmillan Children's Books
a division of Macmillan Publishers Limited
25 Eccleston Place, London SW1W 9NF
and Basingstoke

Associated companies throughout the world

ISBN 0 330 37138 X

3 5 7 9 8 6 4 2

A CIP catalogue record for this book is available
from the British Library

Printed and bound in Great Britain by Mackays of Chatham plc, Kent

CHAPTER 1

DENVER

Twelve-year-old Zack Griffin leaned back at his desk with his hands folded behind his head. His science teacher was explaining the directions for a government-sponsored intelligence test she wanted them to take.

Zack yawned. This class was boring. He couldn't believe the government wanted in on it. His teacher had told the class the government wanted to start a program for future scientists and was testing to see who might qualify.

Zack let his feet drop to the floor and glanced at the first page of the test. It was the usual mumbo jumbo designed to see if his IQ was as high as the school claimed.

In the top corner of the test, where he was not supposed to write, Zack drew a picture of Mrs. Johnson, his teacher. It was a perfect caricature. Two large, square teeth stuck out over her pudgy bottom lip. She looked like a chipmunk with glasses.

"I suppose I should be flattered that you choose to recognize my existence, Mr. Griffin, since everything else in here seems to weary you." Mrs. Johnson stood in front of his desk with her arms folded. "But we do have a test to take, so let's get on with it. Did I mention that if your scores are high enough you will receive an all-expense-paid trip to Washington, D.C., to visit with some of America's leading scientists?"

Zack looked up through half-closed eyelids. "Sounds like a real blast, Mrs. J."

Mrs. Johnson pushed her glasses up and studied the half-asleep boy. She knew he had an IQ in the top ten percent of the entire nation and that he was unhappy "wasting" his time in her class. He would rather be at home working on one of his many inventions. She sighed. "Give it a try, Zack. This one could be different."

LOS ANGELES
"Jeff, would you bring me that stack of government tests from the principal's desk? I need to get those mailed today."

"Sure thing, Mrs. Olsen." The tall twelve-year-old office aide used the secretary's key and let himself into the principal's office. "I don't see them," he called.

"They're in the manila envelope."

"Oh yeah, here they are." Jeff Brown carried the envelope outside and put it on Mrs. Olsen's desk. "What's the deal with these tests anyway?"

The secretary smiled at the boy. "I just do what I'm told. All I know is, students across the country who score high enough get to go to Washington and meet some very important people."

"Really?" Jeff frowned. "It figures. The nerds get all the breaks. How come us regular guys never get trips and stuff?"

Mrs. Olsen raised an eyebrow. "Anyone can take the test, Jeff. If you're interested, there's a blank one in the filing cabinet."

Jeff chewed on the inside of his lip. "Why not? I don't have anything to lose." He went to the cabinet and looked through the files. When he found the test, he sat on the floor next to the secretary's desk and quickly began filling in the circles on the answer sheet.

"I don't want to inhibit your creativity, Jeff. But don't you think you should take the time to read the questions before you fill in the answers?"

Jeff grinned. "No time. Basketball practice is right after school and Coach doesn't like us to be late."

CHAPTER 2

"Excuse me, sir. You need to put on your seat belt. We're about to land."

Zack glanced at the flight attendant and nodded. He fastened his belt and checked his watch. They were fifteen minutes late. It didn't bother him. In fact nothing about this trip bothered him. It was getting him out of class for a whole week.

The plane made a fairly smooth landing and taxied to the terminal. When it stopped, Zack carefully pulled a brown canvas duffel bag out of the overhead storage compartment and unzipped it. The electronic equipment inside looked all right. He'd brought along his latest experiment just in case he needed something interesting to do while he was in Washington.

He backed into the aisle and bumped into one of the passengers. "Sorry."

"No problem." A tall kid about his age grinned at him.

Zack couldn't help smiling back. Then he turned and walked off the plane in search of the baggage carousel.

Twenty minutes later he was sitting near the baggage claim waiting for someone from the Institute of American Science to pick him up. The tall boy from the plane stood nearby, noisily bouncing a basketball while he listened to his CD player.

Thirty more minutes passed. The waiting area had cleared out except for an elderly couple, a family of four, and the two boys.

"I don't know about you, but I'm tired of sitting here." The tall boy had taken off his earphones and was standing beside Zack. "Want to split a taxi?"

Zack scratched his head. "Uh, sure. I guess so. Looks like my ride's forgotten me. I'm supposed to be staying at the Fairmont. How about you?"

"Hey, that's where I'm staying too. Cool. Say, you aren't one of the ner—I mean genius types who won a trip here because of some dopey test, are you?"

"Afraid so. You?"

"It's a long story, but yeah, that's why I'm here too. I'm Jeff. Jeff Brown from L.A."

"Zack Griffin, Denver."

"Great. Need any help with your stuff?" Jeff offered.

Zack shook his head. "I can handle it."

"Okay then. Let's get out of here." Jeff led the way through the lobby. "If we're lucky, maybe we'll spot a video arcade on the way to the hotel."

CHAPTER 3

"How did you do that? Nobody scores that high playing Super Body Crushers on their first try." Jeff lifted his suitcase out of the trunk of the taxi.

Zack shrugged. "I just watched you play and then figured out the game's program. It wasn't much of a challenge."

"Are you kidding me? That's the toughest game there is."

Zack balanced the duffel under his arm and picked up his other bag. "If you say so."

Jeff followed his new friend inside the hotel. "Does everything come that easy to you?"

"Some things don't." Zack stopped a few feet from the registration desk. He eyed Jeff's basketball. "I'm not very good at sports."

"That's too bad." Jeff gave him a sympathetic look.

"There you are!" A short, balding man rushed over to them. "We've been frantic. Our driver somehow missed your flight. I'm Cummings from the Institute. The rest of the group has already left for the laboratory. Let's get you two registered and we'll be on our way."

"Wait," Jeff said. "Don't we get to go up to check out our rooms first and get settled in?"

Mr. Cummings rolled his eyes. "Young man, I already explained that we're late for the tour. Which means we'll also be late for the presentation and the dinner if we don't get a move on."

"But what about our stuff?" Zack asked.

"Don't worry about a thing. We'll leave it with the desk clerk and he'll have a bellhop take it up to your room."

"There's no way I'm leaving my CD player or this ball with strangers. The disk player is brand new and the ball is signed by Charles Barkley."

"And I can't leave this bag. The things in it are too valuable." Zack clutched it to his chest.

"Oh, very well. Keep them if you must." Mr. Cummings moved to the desk to make the arrangements. In a few moments he returned to the boys and rubbed his hands together. "We're all set. Shall we go?" He hurried toward the door without waiting for an answer.

Zack looked at Jeff. "Are you as excited about this as I am?"

Jeff spun his basketball on one finger. "Maybe we can ditch the little guy and go back to Video World. You can show me how to beat that game."

"On one condition." Zack smiled. "You have to show me how you do that." He pointed at the spinning ball.

"Deal."

CHAPTER 4

"And this wing houses some of our most important projects." A tall gray-haired man wearing a white lab coat led the group down a long hall. He opened a door. "In here we have the latest in telecommunications experiments. Feel free to wander around the room and observe, but please do not touch anything."

Zack stopped behind one of the scientists, pulled a small notebook from his shirt pocket, and hastily began scribbling notes.

"I thought we were gonna take off," Jeff whispered.

"In a minute. Some of this stuff's more interesting than I thought."

"Right. Looking at a bunch of wires and glass tubes has always been my idea of a good time." Jeff watched the students milling around the various workstations. They all looked like they belonged here. One kid was actually wearing a bow tie and pocket protector.

"Just my luck," Jeff muttered to himself. "My first night in D.C. and I'm stuck in a stupid laboratory with a bunch of brainiacs."

"Now if you'll all come this way . . ." The gray-haired man led them across the hall. "In this area we are conducting experiments dealing with time and space. Once again, feel free to look, but don't touch."

"Come on," Jeff whispered. "Now's our chance to escape."

"In a minute." Zack moved to the back of the room, where a scientist with white hair that stuck out all over his head was hunched over a table. The man looked suspiciously at the two boys. "Are you interested in time bending?"

"I'm not sure." Zack studied the intricate equipment in front of him. "What is it?"

The scientist cocked his head. "Why, it's re-arranging time, of course. You've seen how light can be turned and sent in another direction through the use of fiber optics, haven't you? Well, you can do the same thing with time—if you know how to bend it."

Zack stepped closer. "How does it work?"

"The subject puts on this headgear, which is attached to the computer, and then sets the clock forward or backward depending on his needs—"

"Dr. Cranium." The tall gray-haired man who was acting as their tour guide spoke in a loud disapproving voice. "You should also tell our guests that these particular experiments work only in theory, not in reality. We wouldn't want to fill our future scientists' heads with a lot of superstition, now, would we? Come this way, gentlemen. The tour will be moving down the hall to view some fascinating work in the area of fats and acids."

"Fascinating," Jeff mumbled.

Zack hung back. "I'd like to get a better look at that machine."

"What? That time bender thing?"

"Yeah. Imagine how great it would be to do something really crazy and then set the dial and go back like nothing happened."

"I knew you and I had a lot in common." Jeff rubbed his chin. "Tell you what. I'll get you back in here later. But when you're finished looking around you have to promise to go downtown and show me how to beat that game."

Zack followed the tour out the door. "How are we going to get away from the rest of the group?"

"Just leave it to me. And be ready to take off when I give you the signal."

CHAPTER 5

"I know you're all anxious for dinner to begin. Especially since the food we will be enjoying this evening has actually been manufactured right here in our own laboratories. But before we get to that, the Institute would like to thank you for coming and make a few presentations based on your academic achievements and test scores."

Jeff caught Zack's eye across the table. Jeff was about to put his escape plan into motion when someone called his name. He looked up. The speaker at the head table was staring at him expectantly.

The speaker smiled. "I guess he's a little shy. Come on up here, Mr. Brown, and receive your award for attaining the highest score ever on the American Institute's intelligence test."

The students were clapping. Jeff stumbled to his feet and hesitantly walked to the front.

When the clapping had died down, the speaker, a serious-looking woman in a business suit, handed him a plaque and shook his hand enthusiastically. "I understand that your best score was in quantum physics, Jeff. Would you be willing to answer any questions the audience might have for you in that area?"

Jeff swallowed. A girl at the first table raised her hand. "I have a question about the submicroscopic mechanical vibrations in the layers of atoms compromising crystals."

The room was silent. Jeff bit his lip. "I, uh . . . well, you see, it's . . . I mean . . . it's sorta like this. . . ."

Zack stood up. "Listen, if you're going to

ask him baby questions, why bother? Jeff is way beyond that stuff. Right now he's working on an experiment that involves electromagnetic interactions with the exchange of virtual particles in gravitational forces."

An excited murmur swept around the room and the audience began clapping wildly. Jeff bowed and quickly found his way to his seat.

Zack winked at him. Jeff nodded toward the exit. When the speaker called the name of the next student the two boys grabbed their things and headed for the door.

Outside, Jeff leaned against the wall and breathed a long sigh of relief. "Thanks for covering for me in there. How did you know?"

"Just a hunch. Anybody who looks at a revolutionary telecommunications station and calls it a bunch of wires and tubes is probably not really into physics."

"Then I guess you're wondering how I managed to win the trip, since I'm not a certified genius like the rest of you."

Zack shook his head. "Not really. However you did it, you were able to pull it off. That takes somebody pretty sharp."

"You're okay, Zack." Jeff stopped in front of the door to the laboratory. "Ready?"

Jeff nodded. "Sure. Because as soon as you get done snooping we're out of here and on our way to the arcade."

Zack slowly pushed the door open. The lab was empty.

They made their way to the back of the room, where Dr. Cranium's experiment was sitting on a glass table. Zack quickly put his bag down and pulled out his notebook.

Jeff watched Zack examine the machine's parts and write furiously. Jeff looked down at his watch and then twirled his basketball. It was still early. The arcade would be open for at least three more hours.

He looked back at Zack, who had typed something into the computer and was now wearing the time-bending headset. "Hey, what are you doing over there? The tour guide said this thing only worked in theory."

"I know. I'm just messing around. Don't worry." Zack set the clock back one minute and flipped the switch.

Nothing happened.

"I wonder what he's overlooking."

"Who?" Jeff picked up a clear fiber rod from one of the tables and looked through one end.

"Dr. Cranium. This machine is amazing but it still needs something to make it work."

"I don't know about you, but I think I hear the arcade calling. Are you finished yet?"

"Almost. Let me just write down a couple more things and we can go."

Jeff came closer to watch what Zack was doing and noticed a small round hole in the top of the Time Bender. He stuck the fiber rod in it and absently wound the hands of the clock backward as he watched Zack write. "This thing looks better with an antenna, don't you think? Makes it seem more scientific."

"What'd you say?" Zack said vaguely, picking up his bag. "We can go now. I've learned about all I can from what's here."

"Good." Jeff moved back to give Zack enough room to take off the headset and get out of the small work space. But when he did, he accidentally leaned against the machine's power switch.

"Whooaa! What's happening?" Zack reached for Jeff's arm. "Stop this thing. I'm . . . I'm disappearing."

CHAPTER 6

Zack was still hanging on to Jeff's arm. But they were no longer inside the laboratory. They were standing beside a sandy desert road.

Jeff's mouth fell open and his basketball thudded to the ground. A strange noise to his right made him jump. It was a large water buffalo—a whole herd of them was grazing on a clump of grass near a river. And in the distance he could see a tall pointed mountain. "I get the feeling we're not in Kansas anymore, Toto."

"We're in Egypt." Zack pointed at the outline of the mountain. "That's a pyramid. I can't believe it! This is all my fault. I set the Time Bender back for one minute in modern Cairo when I was goofing around in the lab." Zack turned to Jeff. "Do you know what this means?"

"We're in big trouble?"

"No." Zack's bag slipped from his fingers. "It means it works. Dr. Cranium's machine actually works! You and I are the first-ever Time Benders. That river must be the Nile, and the city of Cairo must be just over that rise." Zack shook his head as if to clear it. "Just wait till we get back and tell the doctor his experiment is a success. Too bad we don't have time to look around. We could get a souvenir or something."

"Why don't we have time?"

"I told you. We only have one minute. We better stay right here so the machine will pick us up again."

"Uh, Zack, about the machine . . ."

"Get ready." Zack looked at his watch. "It'll be transferring us back any second now."

One of the water buffalo made a contented mooing sound. Zack tapped his watch. "That's strange. It should have picked us up by now."

"What if the machine had a problem?" Jeff asked sheepishly. "You know, what if it decided not to take us back?"

"I guess in all the excitement I hadn't thought about that possibility. You could be right, though. It might be too much to expect the Time Bender to work perfectly on its first try." Zack reached for his duffel. "Don't worry. My dad gave me his credit card. We'll just walk into Cairo and book a flight back to D.C."

"I hope we can."

"What do you mean?"

"It's the machine. You see, just before we disappeared I—"

Thundering hooves pounded up the narrow road and left them in a choking cloud of dust.

"That's weird." Zack looked puzzled as the cloud of dust roared past them. "I didn't know they still used chariots in Egypt. And did you see the way that guy was dressed? He looked like something straight out of the history books."

"I saw it," Jeff said miserably.

"What's wrong? I told you I could get us out of this. It's not like we're stuck here or anything."

Jeff wiped the perspiration off his forehead and looked down the road. Coming toward them at breakneck speed was another small group of chariots, pulled by large black horses. "How much do you know about ancient Egypt, Zack?"

"Some. My dad's an archaeologist and he's taught me a little. Why?"

"I could be wrong but it looks like whatever you know is gonna come in handy about now."

The chariots surrounded them.

A fierce-looking man with huge muscles, a shaved head, and a solid gold band around his arm stepped down. He was wearing a short white skirt with gold braid hanging down the front. The man walked around them but kept his distance. When he had completed his inspection, his chin went up and he folded his arms. "I am General Horemheb, the true scribe, well beloved of the king, the two eyes of the king of Upper and Lower Egypt, vice-regent of the great and powerful Tutankhamen, the chief intendant and the greatest among the favorites of the lord of the Two Countries."

Jeff whispered to Zack, "Do you think we're supposed to clap or something?"

Zack squeezed his eyes closed and then re-opened them slowly. "This can't be happening. It's not real."

The leader raised his arm and two soldiers leaped from their chariots and shoved the boys, forcing them to bow all the way to the ground.

"Feels real to me." Jeff reached for his basketball.

"It can't be," Zack whispered. "Did you hear what he said? He works for Tutankhamen."

"So?"

"Tutankhamen ruled Egypt around 1360 B.C."

CHAPTER 7

The prison door clanged shut behind them. Jeff picked himself up from the grimy corner where the guard had thrown him. "Are you all right, Zack?"

"Yeah. But I just can't believe how wrong this whole thing went. If we had just stayed at the presentation dinner, none of this would be happening."

"Who wants a stuffy old dinner when we can take a ride in an ancient Egyptian chariot? Besides, none of this is your fault."

"What are you talking about?"

"Right before we disappeared I got this brilliant idea to make the Time Bender look better. So I stuffed one of those fiber rods down a hole in the top of it."

"A conductor?" Zack jumped to his feet. "All it needed was a conductor." He frowned. "But that doesn't explain the difference in time, unless—"

"I sorta messed with the clock too. I'm not sure how far back I wound it."

"Well, I guess the good news is at least now we know the Time Bender's not defective."

"Why is that good news?"

"Because if the Egyptians will give us our stuff back, I have a shot at getting us home to our time."

"If we live that long. Look who's coming."

A solemn-looking guard appeared at the door. "The great pharaoh Tutankhamen desires an audience with the lowly foreigners."

"Amazing." Zack grabbed Jeff's sleeve. "I just realized another side effect of time bending. This guy's speaking Egyptian, and somehow we're able to understand it!"

"Great. Then we'll be able to hear for our-selves when the king gives the order to chop off our heads."

The guard unlocked the door. "You will come with me."

They followed him up the same stone steps they'd been pushed down earlier. Only this time they took a different turn and entered a spacious room with golden walls.

On a high platform at the top of three steps, seated on a carved throne, was the pharaoh. He was wearing a blue-and-gold headdress, and around his neck was a golden collar that fanned out over his shoulders. His eyes were lined with black, making them look almond-shaped and somber.

The vice-regent, Horemheb, a group of guards, and three female attendants stood still at the side of the throne. The pharaoh snapped his fingers at one of the women and she began fanning him with peacock feathers.

"There's our stuff." Zack pointed at a pile on the bottom step.

"Prisoners will not speak without permis-sion in the presence of the mighty pharaoh."

The guard pushed them forward. "Prisoners will pay homage to the king."

Jeff and Zack bowed.

A young voice spoke to them. "You have permission to rise."

Jeff raised his head and stared into the face of the pharaoh. He couldn't have been more than twelve years old! "Wait a minute, he's a kid."

"Quiet." The guard jabbed Jeff in the ribs with a wooden spear handle.

The young ruler raised his jeweled hand. "I will allow these prisoners to speak." He gave them a bored look. "First you will tell me what land you are from and then you will explain the meaning of these strange gifts." He pointed to the pile on the step.

Zack inched closer to his duffel. "We have traveled far, Your Highness. Our country is a distant land in the West called the United States. But these things are not worthy enough to be gifts for the great pharaoh. They are our simple belongings. The only gift we have for you is to share our knowledge of life in the West."

"They are gifts," Tutankhamen insisted loudly. He scooted to the edge of his throne with an angry frown. "And you will now explain to the court how they work."

"We better go along with this for now," Jeff whispered. "The kid is starting to get upset."

"But I have to have that equipment or we might not get home," complained Zack.

"Let me try something." Jeff picked up his CD player. "Listen to this, Your Highness."

Before he could get close to the pharaoh, though, the guard held out a long spear to stop him.

"Let him pass," Tutankhamen snapped. The guard immediately moved aside.

"You wear these round things on your ears like this." Jeff placed the earphones over the king's headdress.

"It does nothing," the pharaoh said, pouting.

Jeff turned the CD player on and Tutankhamen's eyes widened. "It is magic! How do you do this?"

"Simple." Jeff hit the Off switch.

"You must be considered a very wise man

in your country. What else can you show me?"

"I can show you how to play the best game in the world."

Tutankhamen sat back, still examining the CD player. "Games bore me."

"This one won't." Jeff picked up his basketball and twirled it on one finger. "I'm gonna need some help to show you how to play it, though, Your Highness. Can you loan me a couple of your guards?"

The pharaoh impatiently waved his hand and two guards set their spears aside and came forward.

"Okay. Here's the deal. You two guys have to keep me from taking this ball and . . ." Jeff looked around. Near the ceiling at one end of the court was a stone ring built into the wall sideways. "It's turned the wrong way, but we'll use it anyway. You guys try and keep me from putting this ball through that ring over there."

The larger of the two guards grabbed Jeff around the middle with one hand and easily took the ball away.

"No. Not like that. Rule number one—you can't touch the guy holding the ball." The big guard set him down. "That's more like it. Everybody ready?" Jeff started to bounce the basketball. The second guard reached for it but Jeff bounced it under one leg and skillfully moved out of his reach.

The young pharaoh clapped. "Very good trick. Now what happens?"

"Now we make a basket." Jeff faked to the left and charged up the middle past the guards. At the end of the court he made a bank shot off the wall through the center of the stone ring. "Ye-es! Brown does it again."

There was a hint of a smile at the corners of Tutankhamen's mouth. "This is an unusual game. You will teach the entire king's guard to play."

"Your Majesty." Horemheb stepped forward. "Do you think it is wise to trust these foreigners to remain in the palace? They could have been sent here as spies."

"Silence. It will be as I command." The king turned to Jeff. "What is your name, magician?"

"Brown. Jeff Brown."

Tutankhamen stood. "Henceforth let it be known and understood throughout the land: Brown Jeff Brown is to be numbered among my chief wise men."

CHAPTER 8

"Pretty nice room the king gave us, don't you think? I mean, just look at the decorations. Who's this statue supposed to be? The guy looks like a crocodile hanging on to a stick."

Zack didn't answer. He had his duffel bag open and was busy taking out equipment. "Look, Jeff, my laptop computer still works."

"Do we have to do this now? I was thinking, since our lives aren't in danger anymore, we could go out and have a look around. I thought we might check out some of the pyramids or the Sphinx or something."

"I don't know. Did you see the way that Horemheb glared at us when Tut made you a wise man?"

"The king'll take care of him. What's he gonna do anyway?"

"If I remember my history right, Tutankhamen only lived into his late teens. When they found the body, his skull had been bashed in. The prime suspects were an elderly uncle, the queen, and Horemheb, who later became pharaoh."

Jeff cocked his head. "Did you say *queen*?"

Zack nodded. "Tut's married."

"To a girl?"

"Of course to a girl. He married a twelve-year-old princess when he was nine or ten. They got married real young back then."

"I'll say." Jeff sat down on the hard wooden bed. "What makes you think Horemheb has it in for us?"

"He just strikes me as the kind of guy who doesn't like anybody to get in his way. To be on the safe side, I think we should get out of here as soon as we can."

Jeff sat for a few minutes watching Zack

hook some wires up to the computer. He sighed. "Since one of us doesn't seem to be of much use here, I'm going to go look around. But don't worry, I'll stay out of trouble."

Before Zack could protest, Jeff was out the door. He found a doorway to an open courtyard and was about to step into it when he saw a girl about his age sneak across the flower garden and stop at the gate. She carefully looked both ways and then slipped through.

Jeff trotted across the courtyard after her and peered over the gate. He saw the girl's back disappear through a door in the side of a large building down the road.

It took two full seconds for him to decide to follow her.

The door she'd gone through led to a dim corridor lit by a single torch at the far end. Jeff could hear muffled voices coming from somewhere in front of him, and he moved toward them.

From out of nowhere a small hand slid into his and began pulling him through a hidden door. He started to protest but the girl put a finger to her lips.

She led him up a flight of stairs to a dark balcony from which they could clearly see the room below. General Horemheb was talking with several men dressed like priests in white robes.

"Isn't it enough that his father was a heretic? Why can't you use that against him? The people will revolt."

"My Lord Horemheb," the oldest priest replied. "As you are fully aware, we are behind your efforts to unseat the boy. Egypt is far too great a prize for a child. The problem is that he is a favorite among the masses. They consider his reign to have brought good luck and prosperity to the land."

"Are you saying," Horemheb stormed, "that you will not help me denounce him?"

"We are merely suggesting, O wise and merciful general, that if the people were to perceive the young king as bad luck they would more readily turn against him."

"Hmmm." Horemheb paced the floor. "We

will start immediately. The work on the tomb will be stepped up and food rations will be lowered. Grain prices will be increased and there will be stiffer penalties for nonproduction."

"Excellent plan, General." The old priest coughed. "And when you have done these things we will step in and blame the boy. His days as ruler will be limited."

"Then, as vice-regent, I will be forced to take over as pharaoh." Horemheb laughed. "And, of course, to assure my position as the new king I will naturally marry the grieving royal widow."

CHAPTER 9

The girl pulled Jeff back into the hall, then led him through the courtyard to a maze of rooms and into a luxurious suite.

"These are my private quarters, Brown Jeff Brown. We will not be disturbed here."

"How do you know who I am?"

"Very few things can be kept a secret in the palace for long. I understand that you are a great magician and wise man from a distant land."

Jeff shifted uncomfortably as he looked at the girl sitting gracefully on a leather chair in front of him. She was gorgeous. Her hair was thick and black and her large eyes reminded him of dark pools.

"The gods must have sent you to help me, Brown Jeff Brown. I am Ankhesenpaaten, wife of the pharaoh Tutankhamen."

"You're the queen?"

The girl nodded. "And now that you have heard for yourself the vicious treachery planned by the king's trusted servant Horemheb, will you aid me in foiling his evil plans?"

Jeff scratched his head. "That's a tough one. You see, I promised my friend I'd stay out of trouble, and besides, he wants to leave as soon as . . ."

A large tear slipped down the queen's perfect face. "I suppose all is lost, then. I will simply have to adjust myself to the idea of marriage to . . . to General Horemheb."

"I don't get it. Why don't you just tell the king what's going on?"

Ankhesenpaaten wiped at her cheek. "It is not as easy as one might think. Horemheb was a great general under the king's father. It was the old king's dying wish that the general become the young king's vice-regent. Tutankhamen would never believe that Horemheb would betray him."

"So the only way Tut's gonna believe the guy is a traitor is if we find some way to expose him."

"We? So you agree to help me?" The young queen gently took Jeff's hand.

"Hold on. First I have to talk to Zack. If he goes for it then we'll see what we can do. But don't get your hopes up. How can I find you to let you know?"

"Don't worry, Brown Jeff Brown. I will contact you."

CHAPTER 10

"Zack, the most incredible thing just happened." Jeff raced into the room and stopped. Zack's computer, which was attached to some sort of mini–satellite dish, was on the wooden bed. Zack's watch was hooked to a clamp, which was connected to the keyboard.

"Wow. You've been busy."

"I think I've got it, Jeff. Not that this system can take us back or anything. The best we can hope for is to try and contact Dr. Cranium's Time Bender and tell it to come get us."

"How soon, do you think, before it will be ready?"

"You sound like you're not too sure you want to go."

"It's not that. I met this girl . . ."

"Relax. There are plenty of girls back in our time."

Jeff sat on the other bed. "It's not like that. This girl is married. In fact she's the queen of Egypt."

Zack folded his arms. "I thought you said you were going to stay out of trouble."

"I'm not in trouble. She is. Or at least she might be if old Horemheb has his way. We sorta accidentally overheard the general say he was gonna get rid of Tut and marry the queen."

"Come on, Jeff. We can't get involved. If we go around changing history who knows what kind of effect it could have on the future?"

"We wouldn't be changing it, just helping it. Besides, I thought you said Tut had a few good years left to rule."

"According to the history books, he does."

"Then what do you say? We do this one little thing and then we can go?"

"Do you have a plan?"

Jeff shook his head. "I was hoping you'd be able to help in that department."

"Why don't you just tell Tut what's going on?"

"No good. The queen says he won't buy it."

There was a soft tap on the door. Jeff hopped off the bed and pulled the door open. A young servant girl stood on the other side.

"My mistress begs me to tell you that the great pharaoh Tutankhamen and his faithful queen, Ankhesenpaaten, will be giving a dinner in your honor this evening. She especially asked me to convey the information that the vice-regent will be in attendance." The girl bowed and left.

Jeff closed the door. "She must think we can use this dinner to expose the general. But how?"

Zack snapped his fingers. "I've got an idea. I just remembered an ancient Egyptian custom. Come on, we've got some quick remodeling to do."

44

CHAPTER 11

"Pass me some of that fruit, Zack."

"What's the matter? Don't you want to try a big hunk of that calf's head? The eyeballs look delicious." Zack laughed.

"Ugh! You try it, then. I'm sticking with food that doesn't stare back at me."

Tutankhamen turned his attention to his two guests. "General Horemheb was just telling me that perhaps we are too soft on our servants. Tell me how they treat slaves in your country."

"We don't have slaves," Jeff said between

bites. "Everybody pretty much takes care of himself where we come from."

"What an interesting idea." The king leaned forward. "And who builds your tombs and temples?"

"Oh, we have workers," Zack said. "But they have good hours and get paid pretty well or they don't work. Of course we know that's the way Your Highness does things here too. I mean, you wouldn't want people to go around saying you're trying to cheat them or anything."

Horemheb's face turned red with anger. "Pay no attention to these foreigners, Your Majesty. They would ruin Egypt with their alien thinking."

"Here's our chance," Zack whispered. He stood and pounded on the table. "Are you insulting an honored guest of His Royal Highness?"

Horemheb was flustered. "I was merely—"

"Sorry, pal. My friend and I take your words as an insult. We challenge you to a contest."

The queen touched Jeff's arm. "According

to our law, the loser of a challenge will automatically be imprisoned for life. Does your companion know what he is doing?"

Jeff swallowed. "I sure hope he does."

Horemheb was on his feet. "I gladly accept. Name the contest."

Zack turned confidently to Jeff and folded his arms. "Basketball."

CHAPTER 12

At either end of the dining hall Zack and Jeff had placed tall poles with woven baskets tied to them.

"Your Majesty, I ask you, has anyone ever been challenged to a . . . a game before? It isn't done," Horemheb sputtered. "Command these foreigners to choose a more honorable contest."

"What's the matter, General?" Zack sat back and watched Jeff bounce the ball a couple of times on the stone floor. "Scared?"

"How dare you?" Horemheb growled. "Very

well. I will beat you at your silly game. And then you will pay for your insolence—"

"Wait." Tutankhamen interrupted. "Since you are the one who made the challenge"—he pointed at Zack—"you must play also."

"Me?" Zack squeaked. "I'm sorry, Your Highness, but the sport of basketball just isn't ready for Zack Griffin."

"Don't worry, Zack." Jeff slapped him on the shoulder. "We'll play them a little two-on-two and wipe the floor with them."

"But you don't understand, Jeff. I'm really awful."

"Enough." Tutankhamen moved to his throne. "You." He indicated one of the guards who had played against Jeff earlier. "You will be Horemheb's assistant. Let the game begin."

"Here." Jeff handed the ball to Zack. "We'll take the ball first. You throw it in."

Jeff moved out to the court. Horemheb stepped in front of him and Jeff slipped around to the outside. "Throw it, Zack."

Zack pitched the ball as hard as he could. It flew wildly over everybody's head. The guard managed to get to it first. He picked it up and held it tightly in his arms. "What do I do now, General?"

"Hurry to the basket and throw it in, idiot."

The guard held the ball to his chest and ran across the court. Jeff and Zack were waiting for him. Every time the guard tried to put the ball in the basket Jeff jumped up to block him. The guard turned to Horemheb. "I cannot, Master."

Horemheb raced down the court and rammed into the two boys, knocking them back against the wall. The guard easily tossed the ball into the basket.

"There." Horemheb wiped his hands. "We are the winners of your stupid game. That should teach you never to oppose the mighty Horemheb."

Jeff stood and tried to catch his breath. "Not . . . yet . . . Your Generalship. Since we don't have referees or a clock, the first team to make twenty-one baskets is the winner."

"Why was I not told of this before we began?"

"And another thing." Jeff took the ball out

of the basket. "You can't run with the ball. That's a different game called football. You have to bounce it the whole time when you go for the basket, and you can't knock everybody down who gets in your way."

"This person cannot be allowed to keep adding rules to this foolish game or it will go on forever," Horemheb said accusingly.

"Are these all of the regulations, Brown Jeff Brown?" Tutankhamen asked.

"There are a few more but I don't want to make it too hard for the general."

"Very well. The game will proceed under these rules and no others. Continue."

Jeff handed Zack the ball. "This time throw it to me."

"Right." Zack waited until Jeff was in position and lobbed the ball onto the court. It bounced up and hit Horemheb in the back of the head. Jeff recovered it and charged down the court, easily making a basket.

"The count is one basket for each side," Tutankhamen called excitedly.

Jeff handed Horemheb the ball. When the big man took it he squeezed Jeff's fingers.

"Let go, you big ape."

"Pardon me, honored guest. I'm sure it was an accident." Horemheb smirked and tossed the ball to the guard.

The guard tried to dribble but his bounces were too high and Jeff stole the ball easily. Horemheb blocked his attempt to move the ball downcourt, so Jeff bounce-passed to Zack. Zack fumbled the ball and sent it flying onto the royal table. Wine splattered all over the queen's dress.

Jeff sprinted over to retrieve the ball. "Sorry, Your Highness. Just remember it's for a good cause."

"I certainly hope so." Servants ran to Ankhesenpaaten to clean her up.

Jeff tossed the ball to Zack, who managed to catch it and quickly pass it back.

"Good move, genius. See, you're getting better already. With a little coaching from me you'd probably get this game down in no time." Jeff took a long shot from center court and scored another basket. "That makes two."

Horemheb and the guard were running all over the court but couldn't keep up with the boys. Zack did his best to stay in their way while Jeff made all the shots. In less than fifteen minutes they had run the score up to 19 to 1.

"I . . . require a pause . . . to speak to my assistant," Horemheb said, breathing hard.

"It's called a time-out, General, and you got it. But don't take too long. Zack and I are anxious to finish you off."

The two Egyptians huddled in a corner while Jeff went to the table for a drink. The queen touched his arm quietly. "I don't like this. General Horemheb is a master of trickery. Be careful."

"He'd have to be a magician to pull this game out of the bag. Two more points and he's out of your hair for good."

"Don't underestimate him. Once he went up against the entire Sudanese army with only a small force and came back victorious—with the Sudanese general in chains."

"We are ready," Horemheb announced flatly. The guard had switched places with him and Horemheb was the one throwing in. He pitched the ball to the guard and then quickly moved in close to Jeff. The guard didn't try to dribble downcourt. Instead he tossed the ball back to the general. Horemheb leaned back and drilled the ball straight at Jeff's face.

Jeff staggered and fell.

"Time-out," Zack yelled. "Jeff, are you all right?" There was no answer. "You knocked him out."

"I don't recall your associate naming this as an infraction of the rules."

"Well, it is," Zack barked.

"I will order my servants to carry him to the infirmary," Tutankhamen said kindly. "We have the finest physicians in all the world. Meanwhile, the game must continue."

"Continue?" Zack whirled around. "We can't continue. My friend is unconscious."

"But it was you who made the challenge, was it not?"

"Well, yeah, but—"

Horemheb threw the ball hard into Zack's stomach. "What is the matter, foreigner? Scared?"

CHAPTER 13

The cell door clanked shut for the second time that day. The guard sneered and shoved Zack inside, slamming the door behind him. "This time you won't be getting out . . . ever."

Zack sat on the cold stone floor, mumbling, "How do I get myself into these things?"

"You know what they say about people who talk to themselves."

Zack jumped up. "Jeff? Is that you?"

"Yeah. I'm in the next cell over. The queen told the royal guard to escort me to prison just as soon as I regained consciousness. I take it the game didn't go so well after I left."

"That's an understatement. Horemheb and the guard made about a thousand points before I could blink. I never even got close to the basket."

"That's too bad. At least they didn't deck you."

"They didn't have to. I told you I was bad."

Jeff sighed. "I wonder what they're gonna do with us."

"According to the books I've read, they'll either starve us or put us to work in the stone quarry."

"Neither one of those would be my first choice."

"Hold it." Zack moved up to the bars. "Did you say the queen gave orders for you to be put here? I thought she was on our side."

"I thought so too. Believe me, I've learned my lesson. Next time we go time bending I'm not stopping to help anybody."

"You sound like you think there's gonna be a next time."

"I have faith in you, genius. If anybody can figure a way out of this, you can."

"Thanks for the vote of confidence. But right now I'm fresh out of ideas."

A large stone at the back of Jeff's cell scraped against the floor and started moving sideways.

"Uh . . . something weird's going on over here, Zack."

"Psst." A small brown hand beckoned Jeff from behind the stone.

Jeff stepped closer. "Who's there?"

"There is no time for questions. Hurry. Follow me."

CHAPTER 14

"I purposely ordered you placed in that particular cell because I knew about the tunnels." Ankhesenpaaten sat at the top of the grayish black steps. "Our ancestors used them to flood the prisons when they became too crowded. My nurse told me about it."

"Your ancestors must have been real nice people."

"Because you have tried to help me, I have made arrangements for my fastest chariot to be waiting at the palace gate. You can get away if you leave now. Travel to the sea.

Horemheb will look for you but I will send a decoy in the opposite direction to give you enough time to escape."

"What about Zack? He tried to help you too."

"I can do nothing for your friend. His cell does not have a tunnel entrance. I am risking my life for you as it is."

"Sorry, Your Highness. I can't leave him. We're in this together."

"Very well." The queen stood. "You are on your own. I will deny ever trying to help you."

"Well . . . thanks for getting me this far."

The queen peered out the doorway at the top of the stairs. Without looking back, she slipped through the door and faded into the darkness.

Jeff ran back down the stairs and squeezed through the opening to his cell. He pushed the stone back, leaving a crack just large enough to slide his finger through.

"Jeff, are you there?" Zack called.

"I am now."

"Where'd you go?"

"Keep your voice low. If the guards hear you they'll come down here. Listen, my cell has a secret opening to a tunnel that leads out of here. Ankhesenpaaten said they used to flood the prison with it."

"Ankhesenpaaten?"

"She was here. Never mind about that. We need to figure out a plan. I could go out the tunnel and maybe come around. I might be able to surprise the guards and—"

"And get your head cut off for escaping."

"You have a better idea?"

"Yeah. Ever heard of Br'er Rabbit?"

"Who?"

"It's an old story about a rabbit that out-foxed a fox. Here goes nothing. . . . *I don't have to put up with you!*" Zack shouted. *"Who do you think you are, threatening me like that?"*

"What's the matter with you?" Jeff tried unsuccessfully to stick his head through the bars to get a better look. "Are you crazy?"

"Guard! Guard!" Zack yelled at the top of his lungs. *"Get me away from him. He's trying to kill me."*

The jailer hurried down the steps and saw Zack cowering in the corner of his cell. "What's going on here?"

"It's that maniac in the next cell," Zack declared. "He says he's gonna rip me apart. You have to do something."

"You called me down here for *that*? He can't even reach you. Now be silent before *I* rip you apart." The guard turned to go back up the steps.

"You mean you're not going to put me in his cell like he told me you would? Oh, thank you, thank you. I wouldn't last five minutes in there."

The guard stopped. He chuckled to himself and took out the keys. "That is a very good idea, foreigner. By tomorrow morning, if I'm lucky, maybe I will only have one of you to put up with." He unlocked Zack's door and dragged him out kicking and screaming.

Jeff stood back and waited while the jailer tossed Zack into his cell.

"Well?" the jailer asked. "I thought you were going to rip him up."

Jeff walked up and punched Zack a straight

shot to the forehead. Zack went down like a stone.

"That's it?" The disappointed guard turned on his heel. "One hit?"

"If I do it slowly it's more fun."

Another guard called and their jailer left them. They waited until they heard him close the door at the top of the steps.

"You were great," Jeff whispered. "I thought I'd actually knocked you out."

Zack didn't answer.

"Zack?" Jeff shook him.

Zack mumbled, then took a breath. "What happened? Oh yeah, you hit me. Hard."

"I had to—otherwise it wouldn't have looked real."

"Next time I'll settle for a little less real." Zack sat up and shook his head. "I can still see stars. . . . Where's the tunnel? We'd better get out of here before he gets curious and comes back and you have to hit me again."

Jeff tugged on the stone and opened the tunnel. "Where exactly are we going?"

"Back to our room. If my equipment's still there I'm going to try contacting the Time Bender."

"What if it doesn't work?"

"Then we better look for a fast camel."

CHAPTER 15

"It'll just take a minute," Jeff said.

"We don't have time. The guard could sound the alarm at any second."

"That ball is special," Jeff insisted. He moved out from their hiding place behind a giant urn. "I'll just sneak it out of the dining hall and then we can go."

He crept up next to the door and peeked around the corner. Everyone had gone and the basketball was sitting on the table in plain sight. Jeff tiptoed over and grabbed it.

"So, you have managed to escape."

Horemheb was standing in one of the side doorways. He pulled a sharp, short sword from his belt. "How appropriate that I shall be the one to catch you."

Jeff edged toward the main entrance, where Zack was waiting. "Wait a minute, General. Can't we talk this over?"

"Only if you find yourself able to speak without a head on your shoulders." Horemheb started for him.

"Run, Jeff!" Zack shouted.

Jeff blasted around the table, trying desperately to keep some space between himself and the general.

"You cannot escape me!" Horemheb jumped, landing in the center of the massive table. "Your fate is sealed."

Jeff slid beneath the table, crawled to the end, and came out on the other side.

"No more games." Horemheb waved the sword.

Jeff raised the basketball over his head, drew back, and slammed it as hard as he could into the general's stomach. Then he ran like mad for the door.

"Guards!" Horemheb choked out. "Stop him!"

Zack led the way down the hall and almost ran head-on into two guards who had heard Horemheb call for help. "This way," he shouted, and ducked into the closest exit.

The angry soldiers stood at the opening but did not attempt to follow them in.

Jeff looked behind him. "That's strange. They're not coming after us."

"It's not strange considering where we are. Look around. We're in the girls' section. The harem."

Jeff stopped running.

Several frightened females dashed behind tall screens to hide themselves from the intruders.

"Go after them!" Horemheb had recovered and was standing in the doorway. "That's an order."

"This way, Jeff!" Zack found a passageway leading to one of the courtyards.

"Right behind you."

They came to two doors. Zack chose the left

one. It was locked. He quickly tried the right. It was locked too. Horemheb and the guards were right behind them.

"Jump, Zack!" Jeff hopped up on the wall and helped Zack over.

They found themselves in another garden.

"Great. Now what?" Zack searched for a way out.

"This way." Ankhesenpaaten was sitting in the garden. She pointed to a passageway. "It leads to my rooms. Brown Jeff Brown will know the way from there."

Horemheb and the soldiers scrambled over the wall.

"Hurry," Ankhesenpaaten whispered. Then she shouted, "The prisoners have escaped! Help!"

Jeff ran through the queen's suite and down the hall. "Here's our room. You fire up the computer and I'll try and keep them out."

He edged the heavy bed over in front of the door and stacked a wooden table and two chairs on top of it.

There was a creaking noise outside the

door. It was Horemheb and his men. "Call the entire king's guard and bring a battering ram," Jeff heard Horemheb order.

"I don't want to rush you or anything," Jeff said, leaning with all his weight against the door. "But we have a little problem here."

Zack wiped his forehead. "I don't get it. I was sure it would work. The satellite dish *should* function as the necessary conductor."

There was a loud thud and the door opened a few inches. "Again! Hit it again!"

Jeff's mind raced. He had been responsible for getting them here. Now he had to do something. His eyes fastened on the crocodile statue. "That's it!"

He grabbed the crocodile and jammed it by its tail into the satellite dish.

The door broke off its hinges and crashed to the floor, smashing the furniture to kindling.

Horemheb stepped into the room.

It was empty.

CHAPTER 16

"Now, if you'll all come this way . . ."

Zack opened his eyes. "We're back!"

A big grin spread across Jeff's face. "You did it, genius."

"It was your quick thinking that did the trick."

"Excuse me, gentlemen, but you're holding up the tour." The guide cleared his throat. "In this area we are conducting experiments dealing with time and space. Once again, feel free to look, but don't touch."

"Do you get the feeling we've been here before?" Jeff asked.

Zack nodded. "The Time Bender must have a glitch in it. We came back earlier than we left. This is the same tour we took before."

The group of students wandered through the room looking at the various workstations.

Zack and Jeff rushed to the back and found Dr. Cranium seated at the Time Bender. He glanced up at them. "Are you the ones interested in time bending?" His eyes traveled to the fiber rod sticking out of the top of the machine.

"He knows," Jeff muttered.

The old scientist's eyes lit up. "What was it like? You found the secret!"

"We have a lot to tell you, Dr. Cranium. The main thing is that your machine definitely works. We traveled all the way back to the time of King Tut." Zack beamed.

"Shhh!" the doctor warned. "We can't tell anyone about this yet. They would try to steal it. I'll meet you later, after the presentation, and you can tell me all about your adventures. Go now. Your group is leaving."

"Right," Zack agreed. "We'll meet you here as soon as it's over." The boys drifted out the door behind the rest of the group.

"He sure is gonna be surprised when we tell him what we've seen." Jeff pretended to bounce a basketball down the hall.

"Too bad you didn't get to bring your ball back with you," Zack said sympathetically. "I feel kind of bad about that."

"Aw, don't worry about it. Someday I'll get another one." Jeff stopped. "Wait a minute. Are we going where I think we're going?"

Zack nodded. "To the presentation dinner."

"Not me." Jeff turned and started back in the direction of the laboratory.

"Where are you going?"

"Back to the Time Bender. I'm gonna try and talk it into taking us to the future. Maybe it'll drop us off at an arcade."

"Us?"

"Sure. You don't want to go to that dumb old dinner any more than I do."

"You've got a point there." Zack hurried to catch up with him. "You know, theoretically, we could spend the whole rest of our lives doing this."

"Why not? I just happen to be free for the next hundred or so centuries." Jeff stopped at the laboratory door. "*Time Benders*—it has a nice ring to it."

GARY PAULSEN
ADVENTURE GUIDE

WRITE LIKE AN EGYPTIAN

The ancient Egyptians had their own unique form of writing called hieroglyphics. They used pictures and symbols in place of words. For example, a picture of an owl was used to represent the sound of the letter *M*. A bow-shaped drill for making fire meant *prosperity*. And a drawing of an index finger stood for the number 10,000.

You and your friends can invent your own hieroglyphics, or secret code, that only you can understand. It isn't hard. First, make up symbols to stand for each of the letters of the alphabet. Once you make up this code, you're ready to begin writing messages that will keep everyone guessing.

Here's one to get you started. Each number in the following message represents a letter. (Hint: The most commonly used vowel is replaced by the number 5.) If you get stumped, turn the page for the answer.

Once you've cracked this code, you and your friends can create your own secret code!

4 5 1 18   18 5 1 4 5 18 19,
   9   19 9 14 3 5 18 5 12 25   8 15 16 5
25 15 21   5 14 10 15 25   20 8 5   23 15 18 12 4
15 6   1 4 22 5 14 20 21 18 5   19 5 18 9 5 19.
8 1 16 16 25   3 15 4 5   2 18 5 1 11 9 14 7.
                  7 1 18 25   16 1 21 12 19 5 14

A selected list of titles available from Macmillan and Pan Books

The prices shown below are correct at the time of going to press. However, Macmillan Publishers reserve the right to show new retail prices on covers which may differ from those previously advertised.

GARY PAULSEN'S WORLD OF ADVENTURE

Danger on Midnight River	0 330 37137 1	£1.99
Grizzly	0 330 37136 3	£1.99
Time Benders	0 330 37138 X	£1.99
Devil's Wall	0 330 37139 8	£1.99
Skydive!	0 330 37140 1	£1.99
The Treasure Ship	0 330 37141 X	£1.99
Video Trap	0 330 37142 8	£1.99
Perfect Danger	0 330 37143 6	£1.99

All Macmillan titles can be ordered at your local bookshop or are available by post from:

**Book Service by Post
PO Box 29, Douglas, Isle of Man IM99 1BQ**

Credit cards accepted. For details:
Telephone: 01624 675137
Fax: 01624 670923
E-mail: bookshop@enterprise.net

Free postage and packing in the UK.
Overseas customers: add £1 per book (paperback)
and £3 per book (hardback).